Keith Baker

Hickory Dickory Dock

Harcourt, Inc.

Orlando   Austin   New York   San Diego   Toronto   London

For my father, Dock

Requests for permission to make copies of any part of the work should be submitted online
at www.harcourt.com/contact or mailed to the following address: Permissions Department,
Harcourt, Inc., 6277 Sea Harbor Drive, Orlando, Florida 32887-6777.

www.HarcourtBooks.com

Library of Congress Cataloging-in-Publication Data
Baker, Keith, 1953–
Hickory dickory dock/Keith Baker.
p.   cm.
Summary: Rhythmic text expands on the Mother Goose rhyme, including a variety of animals
that react as the clock strikes one through twelve.
[1. Mice—Fiction.   2. Clocks and watches—Fiction.   3. Animals—Fiction.]   I. Title.
PZ7.B17427Hic   2007
[E]—dc22   2006003257
ISBN 978-0-15-205818-0

TWP 11 10 9 8 7 6 5 4

Printed in Singapore

The illustrations in this book were done in Adobe Photoshop.
The display lettering was created by Judythe Sieck and Jane Dill.
The text type was set in Kosmik Bold Three.
Color separations by Bright Arts Ltd., Hong Kong
Printed and bound by Tien Wah Press, Singapore
This book was printed on totally chlorine-free Stora Enso Matte paper.
Production supervision by Pascha Gerlinger
Designed by Keith Baker and Lydia D'moch

Hickory
dickory
dock,
the mouse
ran up
the clock.

The clock
struck one...

it's time for fun!

Hickory
dickory
dock.

Hickory
dickory
dock,
a bird
sang to
the clock.

The clock
struck two...

away she flew!

Hickory
dickory
dock.

Hickory
dickory
dock,
a snake
wrapped 'round
the clock.

The clock
struck three...

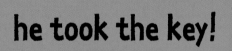

he took the key!

Hickory
dickory
dock.

Hickory
dickory
dock,
a hare
hopped over
the clock.

The clock
struck four...

he hopped some more!

Hickory
dickory
dock.

Hickory
dickory
dock,
some bees
buzzed 'round
the clock.

The clock
struck five . . .

back to their hive!

Hickory
dickory
dock.

Hickory
dickory
dock,
some hens
pecked at
the clock.

The clock
struck six . . .

they chased their chicks!

Hickory
dickory
dock.

Hickory
dickory
dock,
a pig
oinked at
the clock.

Seven

was struck ...

Hickory
dickory
dock,
a billy goat
kicked
the clock.

he rolled in muck!

Hickory
dickory
dock.

The clock
struck eight . . .

he broke a gate!

Hickory
dickory
dock.

Hickory
dickory
dock,
someone
nibbled
the clock.

The clock
struck nine . . .

Hickory
dickory
dock,
a bear
stopped by
the clock.

The clock
struck ten . . .

a porcupine!

Hickory
dickory
dock.

off to her den!

Hickory
dickory
dock.

Hickory
dickory
dock,
a horse
grazed near
the clock.

Eleven
was
struck . . .

she kicked and bucked!

Hickory
dickory
dock.

Hickory
dickory
dock,
the moon
shone on
the clock.

Twelve o'clock
midnight . . .

"Little mouse,
good night."

Hickory . . .

dickory . . .

dock.